To Nathan, Megan, Jonathan, and Andrea,

and to all of my friends and colleagues who work hard and honorably serve our wonderful profession.

I wish to thank attorney Jeanne Seewald for her professional assistance, thoughtful comment, and remarkable insight. I also want to thank Michael Biondo for his creative guidance and endless support.

The book was written to educate children of all ages about the work lawyers do, to improve public perception, and to honor those who admirably serve our wonderful profession.

-Jacqueline J. Buyze

A Story Of Lawyers

Requests for permission to make copies of any part of the work should be submitted online to: jacqueline@astoryoflawyers.com
or mailed to:
Jacqueline Buyze, Esq.,
2430 Vanderbilt Beach Drive
Suite 108-181
Naples, FL 34109

PRT0112A

Printed in the United States

ISBN-13: 978-1-937406-30-1
ISBN-10: 1-937406-30-X

www.mascotbooks.com

Jacqueline J. Buyze, Esq.

illustrated by
Klaus Shmidheiser

By the authority vested in me
under the laws of this country and state,

I Do Hereby Resolve and Proclaim

This book belongs to

____________________________________.

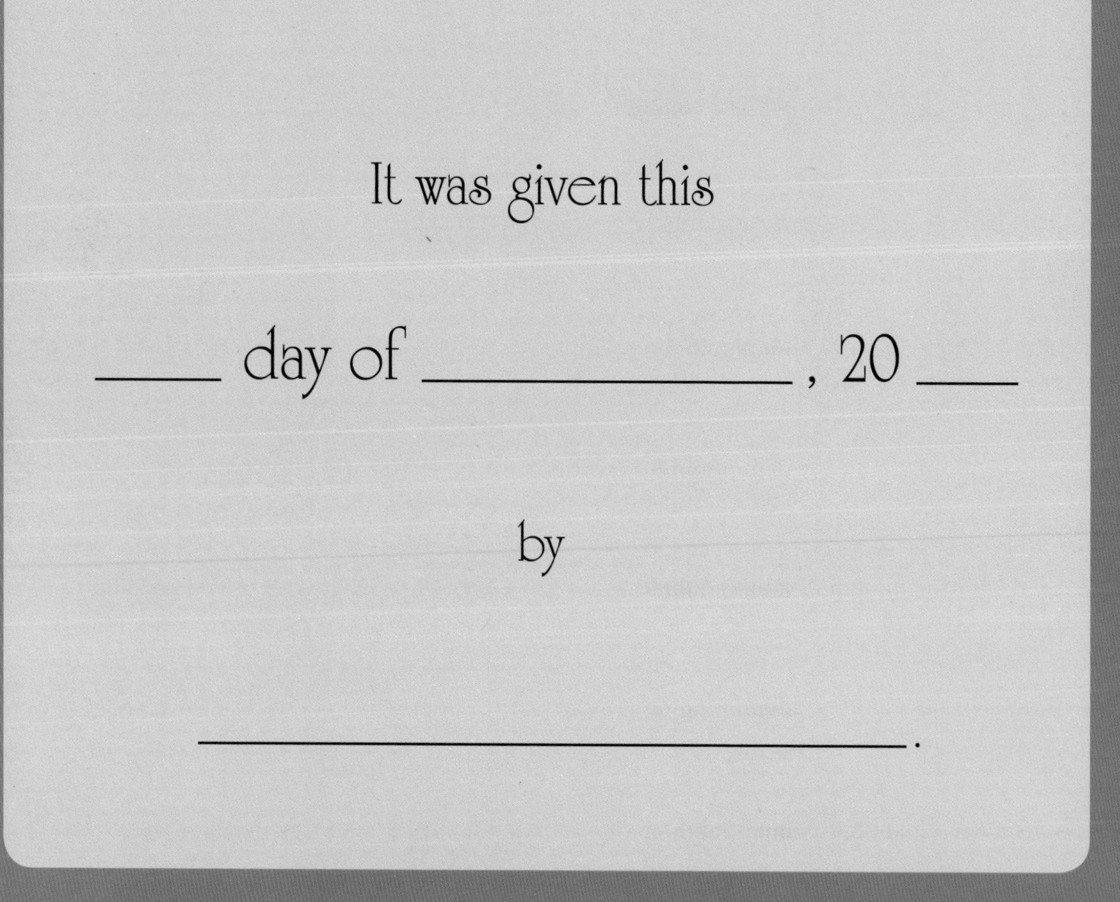
It was given this

____ day of ______________, 20 ___

by

____________________________.

This author's a **lawyer**,
quite proud of it, too.
You will understand why
when you learn what we do.
This short little story
explains it in rhyme.
Please give it a read.
It is well worth your time!

To start, you should know **lawyers** all go to school, where they study intensely to learn every rule.

They then sit for the **bar**, given twice every year,

and must pass this exam to begin their career.

Practicing law is what **lawyers** do.
The work is not easy, and it's also not new.
The law, which is old, is quite **complex** indeed.
And **lawyers** help others comply and succeed!

As for jobs, there are many that **lawyers** can do.
This book in your hands will discuss just a few.
Keep in mind as you read, that the work can be fun.
But in terms of importance ...

it's second **to none!**

Defense lawyers are appointed in court every day.

They ensure that **due process** will not go astray.

If you are arrested, accused of a crime,

a good **defense lawyer** will help ease your mind.

While the list for **defense lawyers** may not be small,
it's a right in America promised to all.

Prosecutors are **lawyers** employed by the State.

They are often in court, and they cannot be late.

Representing "The People," it's their job to protect.

They do this with courage and earn our respect.

When **prosecutors** prove their case beyond **reasonable doubt**, criminals go to jail and some never get out!

Civil lawyers bring cases before judge and jury.
They work hard for their clients and frequently worry.
Resolving great conflicts they did not create.
It can take many years to get things set straight.

Their fees can be steep, as their job isn't easy.
Litigation makes everyone feel a bit queasy.

Judges are **lawyers** who advanced to the bench.
They took a new oath when they left the old trench.
They control the proceedings
and decide many cases.
We rise as they enter
with smiles on our faces.

Judges serve with great honor, and dignity, too.

We all should be thankful they do what they do.

Attorney
of the
Year

Did you know that most **lawyers** do not go to court?

They work in an office with lots of support.

The work that they do is quite different, you see.

But their goal is the same, to help you and me.

Avoiding the court is the name of the game,

and doing this well earns respect and acclaim!

Corporate lawyers help companies buy, sell, and merge,
distributing **options** when stock markets surge.
They get things set up when a deal has begun,
and help wrap things up when a business is done.

S-corps and C-corps and partnerships, too,
these **lawyers** know what all the **entities** do.

Estate planners are **lawyers**
who know how to invest.
Growing your **assets** is what they do best.
They prepare for the future and find lots of ways
to build clients' wealth for their elderly days.

Your money can work really hard for you now.
Keeping it safe is the **estate planner's** vow.

Real estate lawyers
prepare documents and more.
They work well together to complete a huge chore.
When you purchase a house, office, building, or land,
a **real estate lawyer** can give you a hand.

Transactions like these are expensive and tricky.

So when choosing this **lawyer** you need to be picky.

These are just a few things that my **lawyer** friends do
in the hours of their day, far too short and too few.
My friends are all dedicated, a hardworking bunch,
and with work that's unending, they often miss lunch!
With so much to do and not much time to spare,
they still volunteer and show others they care.

If we all did the things laws require us to do,

lawyers would not be needed

and our courts would be few.

But people aren't perfect. We all make mistakes.

We sometimes need guidance when problems grow great.

Lawyers will help you in your time of need.

We promised we would, it is part of our **Creed**.

Lawyers lead our great nation, our states, and our towns.
They advise our officials so decisions are sound.
They serve our communities in numerous ways,
and they do it without recognition or praise.

Hillary Clinton
Yale Law (Class of '73)

So remember our story when at home, school or play.

Be grateful we're here. You may need us ...

Michelle Obama
Harvard Law (Class of '88)

SOMEDAY!

Jacqueline J. Buyze is a Florida-licensed attorney practicing in the area of Alternative Dispute Resolution. She is also a freelance children's book writer. Jacqueline has authored articles on a variety of law-related topics that have appeared in newspapers and professional publications. She has also written personal stories commissioned by friends and colleagues.

Jacqueline received her B.A. in psychology, *cum laude*, from the University of South Florida and her J.D. from Stetson University College of Law. She is a member of the Florida Bar and is certified in circuit civil mediation by both the Florida Supreme Court and the Federal Middle District Court of Florida. Jacqueline has actively volunteered with the Collier County Foreclosure Task Force since its inception in 2008 and presently serves as chair of its mediation subcommittee. She is a former officer/director of the Florida Association for Women Lawyers ("FAWL"), a past president of the Collier County Women's Bar Association, and founding chair of Breakfast & Books, FAWL's nationally-recognized statewide reading and mentoring program benefiting PACE Centers for Girls. She also served for several years as an officer/director of her local PACE center. These experiences were the catalyst for *A Story of Lawyers*, which was originally written to educate her nieces and nephews about the important work lawyers do.

Jacqueline has resided in Naples, Florida since 1986. Prior to attending law school, she enjoyed a ten-year career with the Ritz-Carlton Hotel.

For more information please visit www.astoryoflawyers.com.